Blaze Peppergrove and the Big Race

Blaze Peppergrove Adventures #1

A Short Story By

Lisa Adair

Published by **Books by Lisa Adair**

P.O. Box 834, Rosetown, SK S0L 2V0 Canada
www.booksbylisaadair.com

Copyright © **2023 by Lisa Adair**

1st edition– 2023

ISBN:

978-1-7388299-0-3 (eBook)

978-1-7382558-1-8 (Paper)

1. Fiction, Children's books, ages 9-12, Fantasy, Action Adventure

2. Fiction, Children's books, ages 9-12, Fantasy, Dragons, Mythical Creatures

3. Fiction, Children's books, ages 9-12, Fiction & Literature

Disclaimer:

This is a work of fiction, and unless otherwise indicated, all the names, characters, businesses, places, events, and incidents in this book are either the product of the author's imagination or used in a fictitious manner. Any resemblance to actual persons, living or dead, or events is coincidental.

If you can dream it, then make it happen!

Book Cover design by Milo Adair

"5 Stars. Fantasy, Adversity, Fairy Story—This fun little story is great for kids and teens. It has nice messages about adversity and helping others." Amazon Review.

Contents

In the Beginning

Frowning at the extraordinary lineup, Blaze Peppergrove eased his truck to a stop at the Bridgewater lamp post behind a hot pink Barbie car with two golden fairies sitting in the two plastic seats. He would've charged his truck at the Maple Street lamp post at the other end of the block if he had known there was a lineup here, but he was in too much of a hurry today to complete his deliveries to the various fairy colonies around Evergreen Park. The lamp post across the Bridgewater Avenue expanse into Fern Forest has the closest lamp post with a charging station for Blaze to charge his new customized wheels. Blaze's monster truck is the fastest and easiest way for a wingless green garden fairy like himself to travel around the Evergreen Park block. Blaze climbed out the side window and approached a wood fairy with a clipboard. "What's causing the lineup at the station today?" Blaze asked, running his hand through his green shaggy hair.

"There will be a big race in three days that will take drivers around Evergreen Park following the expanse that borders the block. Everyone is practicing. Here's a flyer," said the wood fairy, hovering just above the ground with her black and blue hummingbird wings, hurrying in a figure eight. "My name is Willow Pollenstorm. If you want to enter your RC in the race, find me so I can put your name down as a driver. The rules and prizes are listed." Willow's brown eyes twinkled with excitement as she handed Blaze a flyer.

Blaze accepted the flyer, skimming the fae script, skipping over the rules at the top of the list of attractive prizes. Besides offering winners silver pieces in winnings, prizes included a flashy Barbie camper with hard plastic sides, GI Joe Soldier Camo Uniforms and a plastic row boat with oars. Still, Blaze thought he might not be able to afford to buy a fairy house for himself, but if he could win a camper, then at least that would keep him more comfortable than the makeshift chip bag tent he currently lived in Juniper Woods with other homeless fairies. "Write down Blaze Peppergrove. I'm going to enter!" Blaze called over his shoulder, walking up to the swamp fairies in the Barbie car ahead of him, "Aren't you a double 'A' battery-operated vehicle? Is it using rechargeables or disposables? I need to charge my truck. My wheels are barely turning because I've been making deliveries to fairies all over the block today. If you aren't charging, then would you mind moving aside?"

"I'm using disposable batteries, but I'm waiting to charge my mp3 player to have tunes to listen to while my co-pilot, Opal, and I win that luxurious Barbie camper! My car is already equipped to pull it." The purple rainbow fairies giggled, fluttering both sets of dragonfly wings. "I only need about an hour to charge it. You can be after me."

Blaze looked up at the sun, trying to gauge how much daylight was left to get through the lineup before him, "I'm going to go home to wait. Could you do me a favour by plugging me in when you are done?"

"Sure thing," she said, smiling at Blaze's handsome green face. "I'm Paprika Cloudystorm, and this is my cousin, Opal Rainbowstripe. We live on this block in the Douglas Fir colony near Evergreen Creek. Are you from the Fern Forest block, too?"

"I'm Blaze Peppergrove. I live across the Bridgewater Avenue Expanse in the Evergreen Park block," Blaze replied, purposely neglecting to mention that he lived in the homeless encampment. "Thanks for your help. Good luck with your race." Blaze quickly turned, leaving the station to cross the dusty expanse known as Bridgewater Avenue. Not looking back until he was on the other side, Blaze ducked into Juniper Woods, where fairies made tents from plastic containers and food wrappers. Blaze picked up dry sticks as he walked under the junipers, thinking about how the silver pieces offered for prizes in the Big Race would help him save for proper fairy housing—waving at a few of his fellow campers adjusting their plastic tarps as he made his way over to where his tent was set up.

Act 1: Into the Junipers

Wolf Turtlewing, a blue swamp fairy with dragonfly wings, adjusted floss stringing up a plastic bread bag around his tent area, called out, "It looks like we will be in for a lot of rain! You better get yourself prepared. It will be a cold and wet night."

"Thanks! I will collect more wood to keep my campfire going before dusk. The owls and other birds of prey will be out hunting in earnest before the rains come." Blaze dropped the sticks he collected into the empty fire pit in front of his tent before scurrying around the junipers for more dry branches. He would focus on getting what he needed to stay warm and dry tonight, then retrieve his truck at the lamp post station in the morning.

The rain began late that night, as Wolf predicted. Blaze's advantages as a wingless fairy are that he doesn't have to worry about keeping his wings dry and is used to walking long distances on foot. He unfolded the flyer to reread the rules. The race is to go ahead tomorrow, rain or shine, cautioning drivers and co-pilots to be prepared for anything, including planning pit stops at lamp posts for charging or changing batteries as needed. Blaze knew that he could drive his truck for thirty minutes before he needed a recharge. That would get him halfway around the block following the expanse before making a pit stop if all goes according to plan. The Big Race is scheduled to start at the corner of Paradise Avenue expanse, across from Rosewood Village, running counterclockwise around the block.

"Are you leaving already?" Wolf Turtlewing asked, coming out of his tent to stand under the bread bag tarp hung over his camp spot. The rain droplets muffled the sounds of other fairies rustling about inside their tents, beginning their daily tasks.

Blaze busied himself, packing a small backpack with food. "Yes, a forty-five-minute walk to the lamppost to get my truck. I will need to test its tires through the muddy terrain to determine if I need any adjustments," Blaze answered as he pulled the plastic he fashioned into a cloak over his head and tucked his felt hat into

his back pocket to keep it dry.

Act 2: A Little Tinkering

It took Blaze almost an hour to walk to the lamppost. The relentless rain transformed the usually dry and dusty expanse into a slippery, soft field of squishy mud. It was challenging to navigate on foot, but Blaze had the experience and strength in his legs from a lifetime of walking. Blaze shrugged, realizing that fairy wings would be useless to him in this wet weather anyway.

The tinker, Thicket, told him that the tires were suited for all-terrain, making it easy to get all around the block at incredible speeds. Because this was the first rain since Blaze acquired the truck, he wondered how it would handle mud bogging and water puddles in the rain, but he wouldn't waste any time trying to find out! He unplugged his truck from the lamp post and crawled in through the side window to begin his test run on his way to Thicket's Tinker Shop.

Blaze leaned out his window to prevent the truck from rolling as he slid sideways through the water-logged ditch, stopping just on the opposite embankment before re-engaging the controls, spinning a few more donuts through the mud, testing the truck's handling capabilities. He realized that the most significant issue would be keeping the windshield clear without any wipers on his way to Rosewood Village on Moon Glitter Pond in the northeast corner of Evergreen Park, where he could have Thicket make some modifications.

He drove under the sweet-smelling rose bushes, stopping suddenly in front of

Thicket Treehop's Tinker Shop in Rosewood Village, where he hoped to make some last-minute modifications to his truck. "Thicket! Are you here?"

"What the devil are you doing out in weather like this?" Thicket chuckled, appearing in the doorway of his shop. "Your new truck is covered in mud! The stickers might come off if you keep that up. I don't know if I can find you another set!"

Blaze laughed, pushing his wet green hair out of his eyes before exiting through the side window of his truck. "I need a few alterations to my truck for the Big Race. I need some windshield wiper, a winch, mud flaps, and something to help me get out of the mud if I get stuck. But I have to be honest with you. I can't pay you until I get more silver pieces."

"That's all right; you will pay me after you win the race!" Thicket slapped his large pink hand on Blaze's back, turning towards his workbench to begin tinkering. "Since you are already wet, you can go back out in the rain to get the supplies we will need. I prefer to keep my wings dry, thank you very much."

Finally, Blaze's truck was ready with all of the modifications. It now had a rubber wiper blade controlled with a hand crank inside the cab and a winch with a plastic hook attached to the front bumper. Blaze also found a container of rope floss, a metal paper clip, and a bundle of sticks behind Thicket's tinker shop that he threw into the truck's box.

"Thanks for everything! I promise to pay you as soon as I can," Blaze called, climbing in through the window of his truck. He gave the wiper blade a few cranks to clear the windshield before engaging the driving controls.

"Good luck and be careful! The rain might clear off, but the driving conditions will still be dangerous!" Thicket waved from inside the door to his tinker shop,

fluttering his colourful butterfly wings.

"Try to stay dry!"

Act 3: An Epic Adventure

The day of the Big Race was attended by fairies of all species (protected in rain gear and large colourful umbrellas) driving various toy cars, trucks, and motorbikes. Blaze flipped the switch control lever to stop his vehicle behind the marked start line. Two fairies struggled in the mud to hold a megaphone to a small podium for the announcer to start the race. A fairy obscured in a green overcoat stepped up to the mouthpiece, "Welcome all fairies to the Big Race. The forecast is for clearing skies and sunshine later today. Even if you keep your wings dry, you will be disqualified for using your wings to fly or help power your vehicles. The expanse on every side of the block is muddy and wet. Drive with extreme caution! Drivers prepare to go on the buzzer, not before."

Blaze flipped his truck's controls to the "on" position, waiting for the countdown. He cranked the windshield wiper to clear away the accumulated water, hoping the sun would shine soon.

"The countdown will begin!" the announcer's voice boomed through the droplets of rain. "Three... two... one..." the buzzer yelled out at the start of the race to the delight of the crowd braving the weather.

Blaze forgot about the slippery road conditions in his excitement, aggressively pressing on his accelerator control. His knobby rubber wheels spewing mud into the air behind him gave him no traction. The tires of a one-seated, red Ferrari F1 car building kit splattered mud onto Blaze's window as it moved ahead, blocking Blaze's view. He cranked the wiper controls a few times before he eased his accelerator controls forward. This time, his tires gripped the mud and propelled his truck forward. He drove with one hand on the steering wheel and cranked the window wiper with the other as fast as possible to clear the mud splattering from vehicles passing in front of him. Blaze grinned, "This race will be an epic adventure!"

As he slid on all four tires around the corner onto the Pine Street expanse, Blaze could see gnomes peaking their chubby bearded faces out of the thorny brambles of Wild Tanglewoods. Suddenly, a donsy of about ten growling garden gnomes bounded out of the tangled weeds, crossing the ditch to throw rocks at the fairy vehicles on the track. A few riders hung out of the windows of their cars, screeching at the gnomes. Blaze bared his fangs, hissing. Seeing these gnomes reminded him of his recent dealings with some burly gnomes from the Wild Tanglewoods. Blaze followed other drivers, trying to steer his vehicle to the far side of the expanse to avoid the flying debris from the gnomes. Once he passed by, Blaze looked over his shoulder with relief to see that the last gnomes were scrambling and tripping over their long beards, retreating from the threatening high-pitched screeches of the fairies driving past.

Checking his battery gauge, Blaze decided to stop at the lamp post on the corner of Bridgewater Avenue for recharging. He hoped that other drivers waiting for the charging station would not try to skip ahead of the line for a better chance of winning the race. As the sun started to peak out, Blaze thought about having his truck fitted with a solar charge panel to avoid having to charge.

Anticipating another slippery turn at Bridgewater Avenue, Blaze purposely slowed down to carefully navigate his truck through the mud. A fairy, completely covered in mud, driving a motorbike pulled out in front of Blaze's truck. When it reached the corner, Blaze watched the motorbike slide on its side into the opposite ditch with its driver rolling behind it.

Blaze slowly eased into the ditch on his way to the lamppost charging station. "Are you all right?" he called down the fairy covered in mud.

Reaching up to remove his muddy goggles, showing a bit of his green skin (the only part of him that is free of mud), the fairy grinned widely, "All part of the fun, I suppose!" He picked his motorbike up, pushing it back onto the expanse, where he scooped mud off the seat before continuing his race.

Blaze had a short wait at the lamp post before he could plug in his truck to charge. Several mud-covered vehicles rolled in after him, forming a long queue. While the vehicle charged, Blaze cleaned the front windshield and ate a snack. He found himself ready to continue the race within forty minutes.

Back on the expanse, Blaze found it easier driving down the middle, where the sun had already dried up a nice trail. It wasn't as dusty as usual, but the tire traction was so good that Blaze pressed his controls to full acceleration. He was almost reaching his top speed of 15 km/hr when he came upon Stone Bridge arching over Evergreen Creek. Suddenly, his truck tires hit a bump in the road. Blaze's eyes widened, realizing his truck was flying through the air! Then the truck landed hard on its two front tires, jarring Blaze's teeth together. *Not a good landing!* Blaze grimaced, trying to steer out of a skid. The truck spun out of control, almost rolling on its side as it spun off the end of the bridge into the swampy ditch, coming to a sudden stop up against a small willow.

Licking away the little bit of blood from his lower lip, Blaze engaged his controllers to accelerate forward. The back tires spun, but he could not get any traction. Reluctantly, Blaze crawled out the side window to check for damage. He sank up to his knees in smelly, grey swamp mud. "Great! I'm stuck in Duckweed Marsh!" he said in disgust. "Good thing I have a winch.

Otherwise, I doubt I could get out of this mess." Struggling to move around to the back of the truck, Blaze used the sides to help pull himself through the sticky mud. Once he could climb up into the back of the truck, he used his bundle of sticks and floss rope to tie around the back tires for more traction. Then he let the winch unwind to its fullest, tied one end of the floss to the hook and the other around a small sapling growing close to the end of the bridge.

Finally, Blaze was able to pull himself into the truck cab. He hit the switch to engage the winch and pushed his accelerator control. The truck was slowly pulled up to the sapling next to the bridge. Relieved, Blaze removed the sticks from the back tires and cut the floss from the sapling. He watched the pink Barbie car race across the Stone Bridge towards the Maple Street corner. Blaze shrugged; I *guess the race is continuing!* He steered his muddy truck onto the expanse to continue his race to the finish line. Mud flew out noisily behind him as it came free from his tires, but it was eventually all cleared away. Finally, Blaze could see the finish line at the end of the street. Fairies were jumping up and down, cheering for all of the vehicles as each one crossed over the

finish line.

In the End

Not far from the finish line, Blaze caught up to the hot pink Barbie car stalled in the middle of the expanse. "What's wrong, Paprika?" Blaze called out his window at the golden fairy.

"I took a chance that I had enough batteries to make it across the finish line, but my last set just ran out. The mud took more battery power than I thought it would," she pouted.

"Hold on! I will push you over the finish line," Blaze signalled for the two fairies to sit back into their plastic seats. He eased his truck bumper up to the back of her car and eased the accelerator forward, pushing the muddy pink vehicle and its two occupants over the finish line ahead of him. The crowd cheered.

"Thanks for the little push!" Paprika beamed, gently shaking beads of water from her dragonfly wings. "Opal and I will walk over to the White Oak Colony to stay overnight and dry our wings. I will fly home tomorrow and get more batteries for my car."

"Excuse me, I would like to thank you for checking to see if I was all right when I slid off the road," the motorbike driver covered in mud approached Blaze. "I am Bard Hemlock, winner of the Barbie camper. I wondered if I could hire you to tow the camper to Cat Tail Colony. I can pay you five silver pieces out of my winnings."

"Yes, I can, but not until tomorrow. I have to recharge before towing it. It won't take long if the Maple Street expanse dries up more. Which fairy house is yours?" Blaze smiled, knowing that this job would earn enough silver pieces to pay the Tinker Thicket for the recent modifications to his truck and one or two for himself.

"We are in the stick-build with the blue pebble chimney and moss roof. There will be wee fairies fluttering about. You can't miss it!" Bard grinned. "It sure was fun to slide around in all that mud today! I can't wait to tell my growing family we will expand the house! Expect my partner to feed you when you arrive!" He laughed, slapping Blaze on the shoulder, leaving a big muddy handprint as he walked away.

Blaze reflected on his day. He didn't win the Big Race, but he was satisfied to learn by experiencing the epic adventure: always be prepared, mudding takes more power, and always stop to help others whenever possible. He jingled the silver pieces in his leather pouch, hoping to make his delivery tomorrow afternoon.

The End.

Please take a moment to write an honest review of this story on Amazon or Goodreads. Thank you!

Blaze will continue his adventures in *Blaze Peppergrove and the Tangled Web, Blaze Peppergrove Adventures #2.* Visit the website to subscribe to the monthly newsletter for short story fantasy adventures and get all the latest on Blaze Peppergrove and its characters. From time to time, newsletter subscribers will receive unique bonus pages. **Sign Up!**

Blaze Peppergrove Adventures Story Blurbs

Blaze Peppergrove is a thrill-seeking, wingless fairy determined to fulfill his dreams in Evergreen Park. He has left his family and life as a garden fairy to seek adventure and fortune on his terms. Living in the homeless fairy camp under the juniper trees isn't easy, but Blaze meets different fairies while working odd jobs to earn silver pieces.

#0 Blaze Peppergrove to the Rescue

After a disappointing job interview at the biggest fairy employment agency, Blaze decides to risk everything by taking on the rescue of a missing fairy in exchange for the lucrative reward offered—hoping this will be enough to start his own business to secure his financial independence, he must first navigate the dangers along the way.

#1 Blaze Peppergrove and the Big Race

With the promise of a big payoff, Blaze thinks his luck is about to change when he signs up for a big race around the block promising luxurious prizes; unfortunately, lousy weather creates more obstacles to overcome than expected.

#2 Blaze Peppergrove and the Web of Lies

In the city's heart, cloaked in shadows and secrets, two homeless fairies of Evergreen

Park, Blaze and Wolf, stumble upon an unusual opportunity that plunges them into a realm of stolen silver and harrowing escapes. Little do they know, this adventure will reveal the heroes within, pit them against relentless criminals, and illuminate the profound worth of their friendship. Will their extraordinary journey rewrite their destinies and reshape Juniper Woods' future?

This adventure is coming soon! See the author's website for details: https://www.booksbylisaadair.com

About the Author

 Author Lisa Adair grew up in a small town in the forestry region of northern Saskatchewan. With an English and Science degree and a love of the mystery genre, mainly when it showcases positive role models on journeys of self-discovery, she looks forward to continuing her examination of Evergreen Park and its colourful fairy characters with the Blaze Peppergrove Adventures, which she introduced with *Blaze*

Peppergrove to the Rescue (2023), inspired by her love of mythical creatures. She is also the author of the adult mystery novel *The Puzzle Box* (2023), which kicked off the series *The Glenmere Box Mysteries*.

When Lisa is not writing, painting, scrapbooking, or playing the guitar, she enjoys camping and hiking in and around beautiful Saskatchewan, where she lives with her husband, teenage children, and the family's beloved rescue dog.

To connect with the author, visit:

http://linktr.ee/booksbylisaadair

https://www.booksbylisaadair.com

Adair/Blaze Peppergrove and the Big Race

Subscribe to a monthly newsletter!

To subscribe to a monthly newsletter, visit http://www.booksbylisaadair.com

About the Cover Artist

Artist Milo Adair is currently employed as a gallery assistant. He enjoys exploring art mediums and using markers, ink and watercolours to draw his favourite superhero characters, especially Spidey-guy.

To follow the artist or commission artwork, visit **http://instagram.com/milosartstudio** or **http://tiktok.com/@the5thghostbuster**